LEARN POTHWARI
With The Nana G
SHOW
The Pahari Alphabet

Written by Tehseen Jay

Copyright

No part of this publication may be reproduced, stored in a retrieval system, or transmitted in any form by any means, electronic, mechanical, photocopying, recording or otherwise without the prior permission of the publishers.

Published in 2022
By The Nana G show Ltd.
Copyright © 2022
All rights reserved

A

Nana G is sat with an aunty wearing ainka eating an anda.

Ainka (glasses)
Anda (egg)

B

Nana G is brushing the bakri's baal and the bakri is wearing a benain.

Bakri (goat)
Baal (hair)
Benain (vest)

C

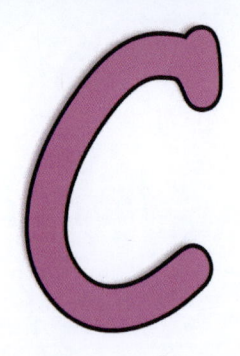

The churail scared the chor with her chappal.

Churail (ghost)
Chor (thief)
Chappal (slipper)

D

The **daaku** drove away with Nani G's **dand** in the dark.

Daaku (bandit)
Dand (teeth)

E

Ejaz is eating an ellachi on Eid.

Ellachi (cardamom)

F

Farzand is feeling **faar** in her stomach after having **falooda**.

Faar (stomach-ache)
Falooda (a dessert)

G

Ghafoor is eating gobi in his gandhi gaddi.

Gobi (cauliflower)
Gandhi (dirty)
Gaddi (car)

H

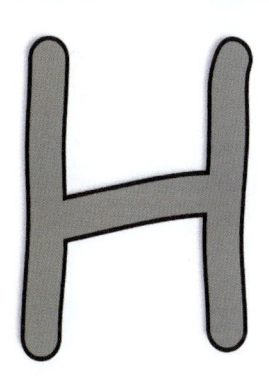

Hairy haathi put a haddi in the halva.

Haathi (elephant)
Haddi (bone)
Halva (a dessert)

I

Iqbal is doing isthri and eating an ice cream in an igloo.

Isthri (iron)

J

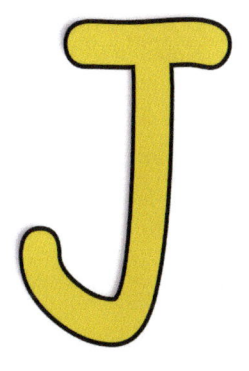

The jaanvar are jumping like junglees in the jaaz.

Jaanvar (animals)
Junglee (hooligan)
Jaaz (aeroplane)

K

The khotha is eating a khakree wearing a kaacha in a koti.

Khotha (donkey)
Khakree (melon)
Koti (house)

L

Leyla has lost his laal lota.

Leyla (lamb)
Laal (red)
Lota (water can)

?

M

Mubushra is applying makeup on a maalta in the mela.

Maalta (orange)
Mela (funfair)

N

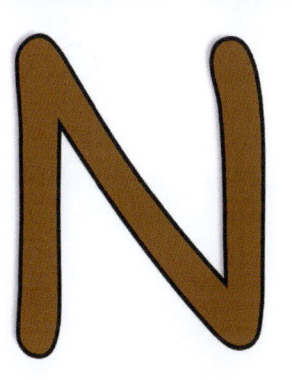

Nana Gs' nava naara fell in the nihari.

Nava (new)
Naara (trouser string)
Nihari (lamb shank curry)

O

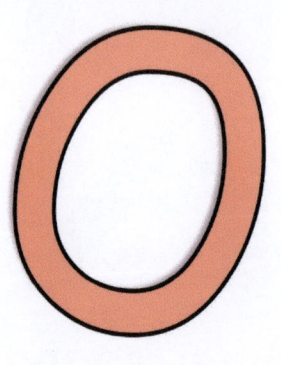

Osman's ostrich ate the ojri.

Ojri (stomach curry)

P

Gahfoor is learning Pahari with his **pehn pra** wearing a **patti-vi pent** from **Pindi**.

Pehn (sister)
Pra (brother)
Patti-vi Pent (ripped jeans)
Pindi (Rawalpindi)

Q

The Queen is hosting a quiz in the qila.

Qila (fort / castle)

R

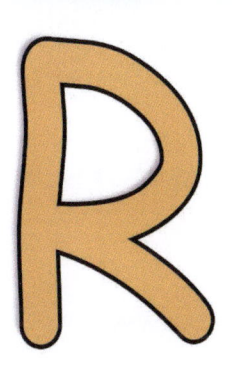

Tariq is opening his roza with roti in Ramadan.

Roza (fast)
Roti (chapati)

S

Dadi G is sat on a sap eating semiya.

Sap (snake)
Semiya (vermicelli / dessert)

T

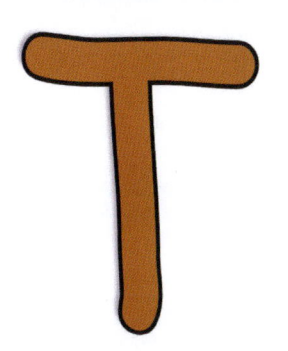

The tamuri chased Tehseen up the tree.

Tamuri (wasp)

U

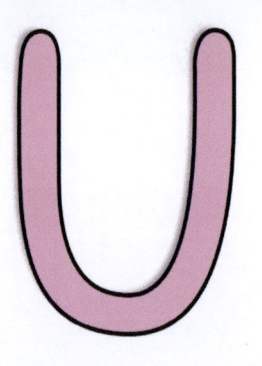

The ustad teaches Tariq Urdu sitting on a unicorn.

Ustad (teacher)

V

Nani G came **vapas** and vacuumed inside Vaqas's van.

Vapas (back)

W

Dada G attends Waseem's **walima** in a white wagon.

Walima (wedding party)

X

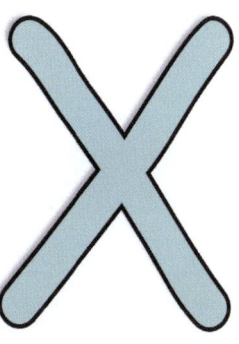

Nani G goes to the hospital for an X-ray.

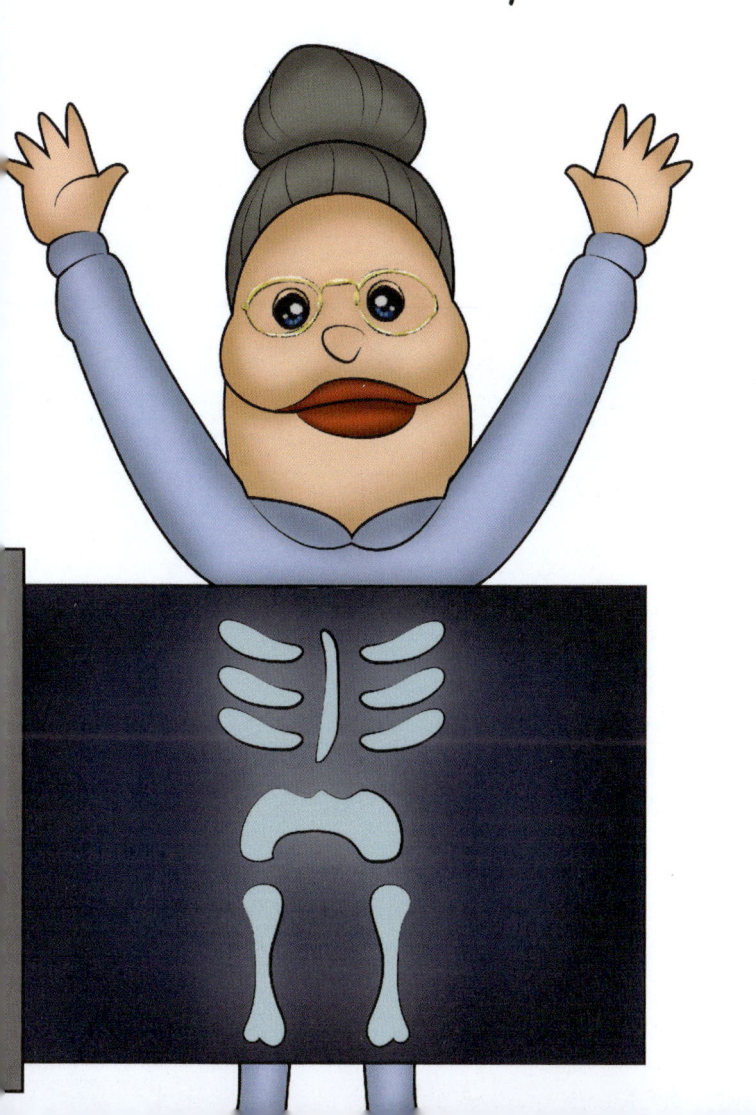

Y

Yaqoob is making yakhni for Yasmin in his yellow yacht.

Yakhni (stew / soup)

Z

Gahfoor steals Zainab's zaytoon na tehl.

zaytoon na tehl (olive oil)

ABOUT US

Tehseen Jay is a British Pakistani who was raised in the bustling city of Bradford, by both of his grandparents. Tehseen is the creator of the notorious Nana G show brand which first launched in 2017. The brand aims to celebrate and promote the potwari dialect within the South Asian Community.